Maezie's Pumpkin Patch

based on a true story

written by

Lynn Martin Snowden

illustrated by

Kyle Sydney Powell

 Petunia Publications

2014

The text of this book is set in Garamond.
The illustrations are acrylic wash with pen.

ISBN 978-0-9914929-0-9

Printed in the U.S.A.

For Mae with love

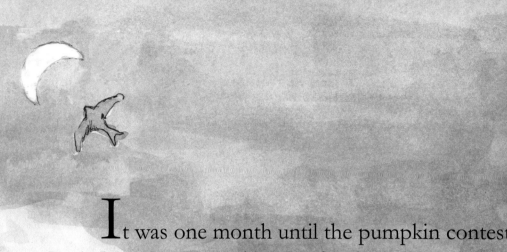

It was one month until the pumpkin contest, and Maezie was working hard in her patch making sure all of her pumpkins were the biggest they could be. This year she was dreaming of a winner.

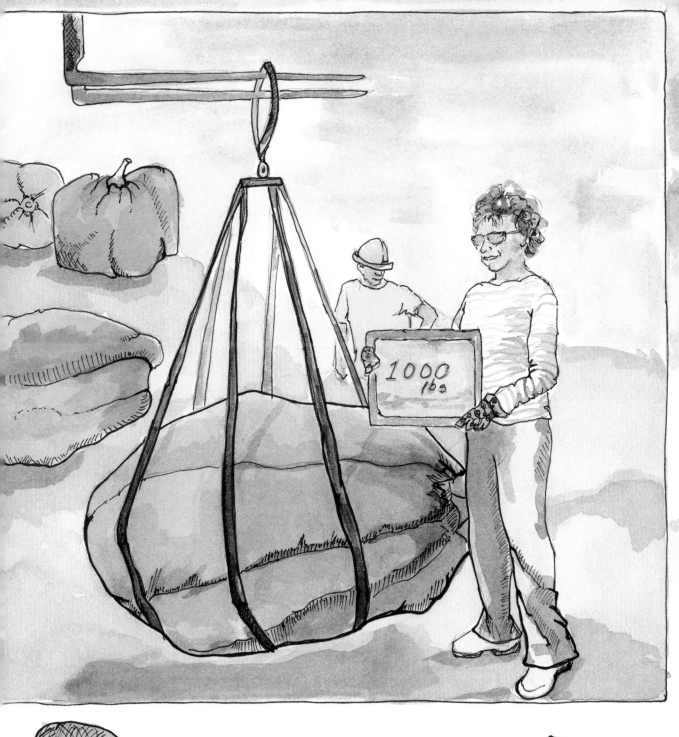

Every day Maezie worked in her
garden watering, weeding,

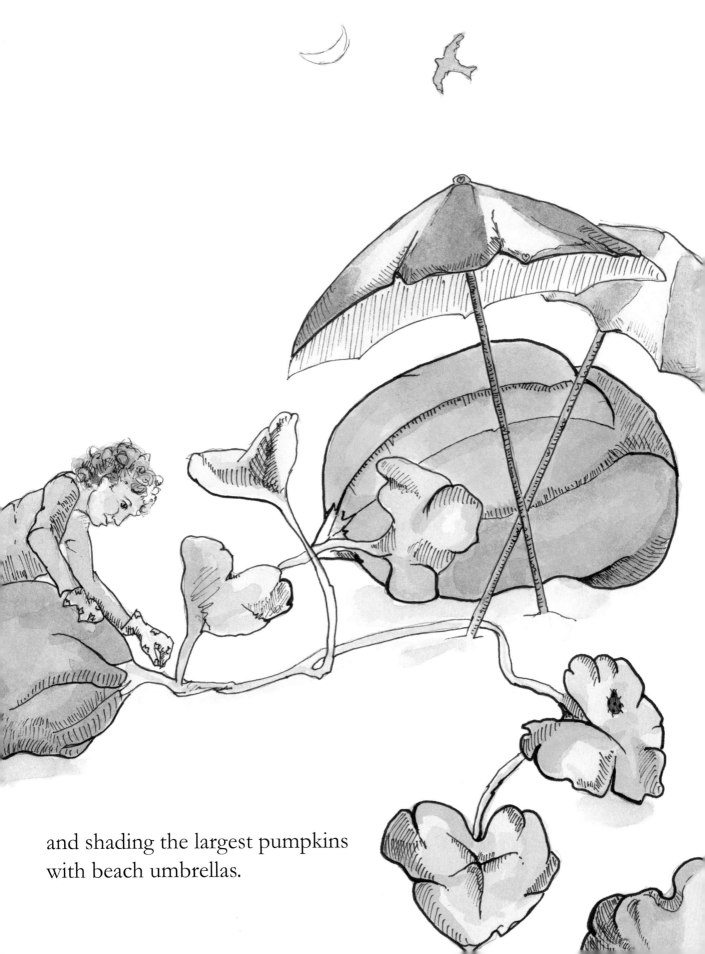

and shading the largest pumpkins
with beach umbrellas.

All the neighbors loved Maezie's pumpkin patch. They watched her grow her pumpkins year after year. And every year the pumpkins brought so much joy to the whole neighborhood.

One autumn morning, Maezie went out to pick tomatoes and check on her pumpkins.

To her dismay, she found her pumpkin patch ransacked and looted. She was shocked. She had worked in her pumpkin patch for months, and now all of the pumpkins were stolen, smashed, or broken. Because the largest pumpkin was too heavy to lift, the thieves had stabbed it with the beach umbrellas.

Maezie was heartbroken, and she began to cry. As she stood in her garden, neighbors came out to begin the day and saw the devastation. Pumpkins and seeds were strewn from one side of the street to the other.

One neighbor said that she would call the paper
to report the news. Another said he would call the
local television station; he even offered a reward in
order to find the culprits of such a crime.

By afternoon, Maezie had newspaper and television reporters in her garden. The entire community, including the fire captain and school crossing guard, arrived to support her.

Her picture made the headlines of the city paper, and her story aired on both local and national news. Maezie vowed that she was not going to let the thieves stop her from growing her magnificent orange and yellow pumpkins.

In the months that followed, Maezie dried the pumpkin
seeds that she was able to save and prepared the soil
for a new patch.

When the time came in the spring to plant the
seeds, everyone in the neighborhood helped her.
Happily, she gave each one of them some of her
extra pumpkin seeds so that they, too, could grow
a pumpkin patch of their own.

By pumpkin harvest time, Maezie's garden was filled with prizewinning pumpkins, and the entire neighborhood had a glow of orange.

As Maezie and her neighbors stood and admired their hard work, they all began to laugh. They had created a sea of pumpkins so enormous that no pumpkin thief would ever venture into their neighborhood again.

Author's Note

The inspiration for writing a story about a ransacked pumpkin patch came from a real incident that happened on August 31, 2012. After six months of toil, Maezie's patch was destroyed. The thieves were never caught. However, Maezie's touching story was seen nationwide, and she received condolences from friends and strangers both young and old. With compassion and love from so many, Maezie found the strength needed to cultivate a new patch of pumpkins.

About Maezie

Raised in sunny Southern California, Maezie Powell has loved gardening for as long as she can remember. As a child, she would help her father dig holes among the vegetables and delight in watching the chickens run around her ankles in search of unearthed worms.

When she moved to a home of her own, Maezie began to plant---flowers and succulents and fruit trees and vegetables. Just a few years ago, she decided to add a pumpkin patch to her glorious garden. For eight dollars she purchased a giant pumpkin seed from a man in Nova Scotia. That one seed produced a pumpkin that weighed over three hundred pounds. With her tremendous success a newfound passion grew into what some might call pumpkin mania.

Maezie, a remarkably youthful ninety-five-year-old, gives her pumpkin seeds to all who are interested in creating a pumpkin patch of their own. And, each autumn, she donates her white, green, yellow, and orange prizewinning pumpkins to the Children's Garden at the Huntington Library in San Marino, California.

Maezie's Pumpkin Growing Tips

Select a Planting Site

Pumpkins grow best in direct sunlight, so an area that receives 8 hours of sunlight a day is ideal.
Planting should be done when the danger of frost has passed and the soil has thoroughly warmed.

Prepare the Soil

The best pumpkins come from soil that is well-prepared.
Dig a hole about 36 inches deep and 3-5 feet in diameter.
Mix the soil with about 5-6 bags of soil amendments.
Put all the soil back in the hole.
You should have a mound that is 2-5 feet in diameter and 16-18 inches high at the center.

Planting the Seeds

Soak the seeds in water overnight.
Plant three seeds in a flat, horizontal direction two inches from the surface in the middle of the mound.
Planting in the late afternoon or early evening is best.
Then, water the soil thoroughly.
You may wish to protect the seeds from wind and strong sunlight by placing an open cardboard box around the seeds until they get established, which takes about 7-10 days.

Watering

Pumpkins are 90% water, so the soil should be kept moist.
Watering daily in the early morning or late afternoon is
best.
When the pumpkin is the size of a small ball, you may wish
to carve your name in the skin. As the pumpkin gets larger,
your name will stretch and grow!

Picking the Pumpkins

Pumpkins are ready for harvest once the fruit is deep
yellow or fiery orange, depending on the variety.
Cutting the pumpkins from the vine and leaving several
inches of the stem attached helps the pumpkins stay fresh.
Let the pumpkins stand in the sun for 10 days and then
store the harvest in a cool, dry place.

Maezie's Favorites

Cinderella

Sugar

Baby Boo

Turban

Jarrahdale

Golden Nugget

Gourds

Cheese

Jack-O'-Lantern